Sămmỹ
THE SEĀL

Story and pictures by **Syd Hoff**

HarperTrophy®
A Division of HarperCollins*Publishers*

SAMMY THE SEAL
Copyright © 1959 by Syd Hoff
Copyright renewed 1987 by Syd Hoff
All rights reserved. No part of this book may be used or reproduced in any manner
whatsoever without written permission except in the case of brief quotations
embodied in critical articles and reviews. Printed in the United States of America.
For information address HarperCollins Children's Books, a division of
HarperCollins Publishers, 10 East 53rd Street, New York, NY 10022.

Library of Congress Catalog Card Number: 59-5316
ISBN 0-06-022525-4
ISBN 0-06-022526-2 (lib. bdg.)
ISBN 0-06-444028-1 (pbk.)

Sammy
THE SEAL

It was feeding time at the zoo.

All the animals

were getting their food.

7

The lĭŏns ātĕ thĕĭr mēat.

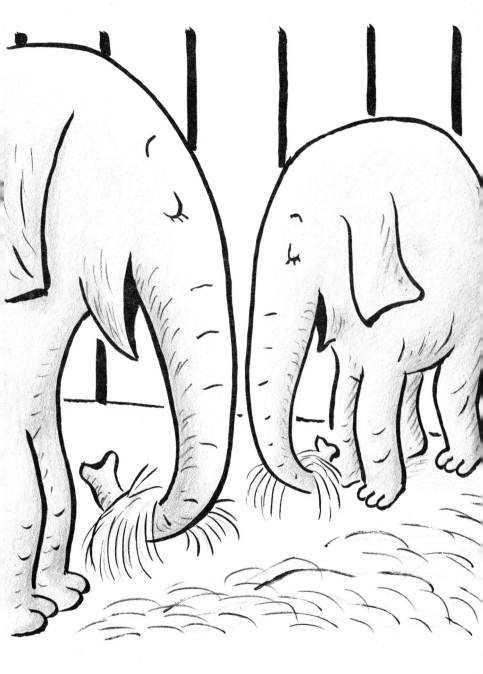

The ĕlĕphắnts āte thĕir hāy.

The mŏnkēys āte thĕir bănănăs.

The bĕars āte thĕir hŏnēy.

Thĕn ĭt wăs timĕ
fōr the sēals to bē fĕd.
Mr. Jŏhnsŏn took thĕm fĭs<u>h</u>.

12

"Hooray for fish!" said the seals.

They jumped in the water.

Soon the basket was empty.

"That is all there is," said Mr. Johnson.

"There is no more."

"Thank you for the fish," said the seals.

"They were good."

The seals were happy.

Bŭt one lìttlĕ sēal wăs nŏt hăppȳ.

Hē săt bȳ hìmsĕlf.

Hē lookĕd săd.

"What ĭs wrŏng, Sămmȳ?"

said Mr. Jŏhnsŏn.

16

"Ī wănt to know
what ĭt ĭs līke
ŏutsīde the zoo," said the lĭttle sēal.
"Ī wănt to gō out ănd look ăround."

17

"All right, Sammy," said Mr. Johnson.

"You have been a good seal.

You may go out and see."

"Good-bye, Sammy," said the other seals.

"Have a good time."

"Good-bye," said Sammy.

"Where are you going?" said the zebra.

"I am going out," said Sammy.

"Have fun," said the hippo.

"Come back soon," said the giraffe.

Sammy walked and walked and walked.

He did not know what to look at first.

"That seal must be from out of town,"
said a man.

Sammy looked at everything.

"What street is this?" said a man.

"I am a stranger here myself,"
said Sammy.

"I guess it is feeding time here, too,"
said Sammy.

"That is a lovely fur coat," said a lady.

"Where did you get it?"

"I was born with it," said Sammy.

28

"I wish I could find some water.
I am hot. I want to go swimming,"
said Sammy.

"We are sorry. There is no room for you in this puddle," said the birds.

"And there is no room for you here,"
said the goldfish.

"Keep out," said the policeman.

"You cannot swim in there."

"Ah, here is a place!" said Sammy.

"Who is in my bathtub?" said someone.

"I am sorry," said Sammy.

He left at once.

Some children were standing in line.

Sammy got in line, too.

"What are we waiting for?"

asked Sammy.

"School. What do you think?" said a boy.

"That will be fun.

I will come, too," Sammy said.

The teacher was not looking.

Sammy sat down.

The children made words with blocks.

Sammy wished he could spell.

"All right, children.

Now we will all sing a song,"

said the teacher.

The children had good voices.

"That sounds fine," said the teacher.

"But one of you is barking—

just like a seal."

"Is it you, Joey?"
said the teacher.
"No," said Joey.

"Is it you, Helen?"

said the teacher.

"No," said Helen.

45

"Is it you, Dorothy, Robert, Fred, Joan, or Agnes?"

"No," said the children.

"Then it must be you,"

said the teacher.

"I am sorry. This school is
just for boys and girls."

48

"Please let me stay," said Sammy.

"I will be good."

"All right. You may stay,"

said the teacher.

Sammy was happy.

He sat at his desk

and looked at the teacher.

50

He learned how to read.

He learned how to write.

"And now it is time to play,"
said the teacher.

"Who wants to play a game?"

"We do," said the children.

They threw the ball over the net.

"The ball must not hit the ground,"
cried Sammy's team.

"Somebody catch the ball."

Sammy caught the ball on his nose!

A boy on the other team tried
to catch the ball on his nose, too.
"Boys must catch with their hands,"
said the teacher.

Sammy tried to catch the ball
with his flippers.

"Seals must catch with their noses,"
said the teacher.

58

Up and down went the ball,

from one side to the other.

At last the teacher blew her whistle.

"Who wins?" said the children.

"It is even," said the teacher.

Everybody was happy.

A bell rang. School was over.

"Will you be here tomorrow?"

said the children.

"No," said Sammy.

"School is fun,

but I belong in the zoo.

I just wanted to know

what it is like outside.

Now I have to go back."

"Good-bye, Sammy," said the children.

"We will come to see you."

"Good," said Sammy.

Sammy was in a hurry

to get back to the zoo.

He had so much to tell the other seals.

"May I welcome you home, Sammy,"

said Mr. Johnson.

"I am glad you are back.

You are just in time for dinner."

"There's no place like home,"
said Sammy.